A

a Boyfriend
& a Side Dude

Tanisha Stewart

A Husband, a Boyfriend, & a Side Dude

Copyright © 2018 Tanisha Stewart

Books may be purchased in quantity and for special sales by contacting the publisher, Tanisha Stewart, by email at tanishastewart.author@gmail.com.

Cover Design: Tanisha Stewart
http://www.tanishastewartauthor.com

Editing: Janet Angelo
https://indiegopublishing.com/

First Edition

Published in the United States of America

by Tanisha Stewart

Dedication

I dedicate this book to God and to my friends, family, and readers, and to my amazing newfound group of writers, Big Black Chapters (Facebook). This group has truly been a blessing in my life, as it sparked the idea within me to create these Quick Reads.

To the Reader

If you enjoy this Quick Read, please know that I appreciate so much a positive review on Amazon.

Also, if you would like to read more of my work, or hear more about me as an author, feel free to join my email list at https://www.tanishastewartauthor.com/contact, or follow me on social media:

Facebook: Tanisha Stewart, Author
Instagram: tanishastewart_author
Twitter: TStewart_Author

A Husband
a Boyfriend
& a Side Dude
Tanisha Stewart

Chapter 1

I pulled up to La Casa Royale, a restaurant my best friends Rachel and Natasha and I often frequented. I immediately spotted both of their vehicles, which meant I was late – again. I scrambled to get out of my car and up to the hostess so I could figure out where we were seated. The place looked packed already, which was kind of unusual for a Sunday. *They must have some kind of event going on that I don't know about.*

"Ce'Anna?" The hostess, Becky, said with a smile.

"Oh, how did you know?" I studied her features to see if I knew her from somewhere.

"Your friend Rachel described you to a T."

I chuckled. "That's Rachel for you – so detailed."

I followed as she led me to where Rachel and Natasha were seated with their drinks. As soon as she walked away, Natasha started in on me.

"Girl, what took you so long? You said you would be here at least half an hour ago!"

I opened my mouth to formulate a lie, but it took me a second. I certainly couldn't say, *With your man*, so I pulled an excuse out of my ass.

"Girl, the traffic was crazy getting here. Why is it so packed on a Sunday?"

Natasha's eyes told me she accepted my explanation, but Rachel's expression said otherwise. I quickly glanced away from her and busied myself with the menu. The last thing I needed was more questions, and I was already clearly a terrible liar.

"Girl, so how are things with Trent?" said Natasha.

"We're good," I said without looking up. "He still wants a baby."

"You need to give him one soon. I am *so* looking forward to being where you guys are in your relationship."

I knew my face had to be blushing crimson by now. I needed out of this situation.

"What's been up with Xaveon?" said Rachel. I caught her glance before she focused on Natasha.

"Things are really going good!" Natasha beamed. "I think he might be 'the one'. He's so chill, and so understanding."

I almost opened my mouth to agree with her, but then I remembered exactly why that was a horrible idea.

"That is so good to have a man you can *trust*." Rachel shot another glance in my direction that Natasha didn't catch, but I sure did.

Does she know? Or am I just paranoid?

I definitely needed an exit strategy ASAP.

My phone buzzed with a notification from Trent.

What time you coming home? Did you forget about movie night?

My jaw dropped. Trent and I scheduled a date night in front of the TV screen every Sunday, no matter what, because we wanted to ensure that we spent enough time together despite our busy schedules. I felt like a complete jerk for forgetting.

"Ooh, Rachel, Natasha, I gotta go." I hurried to my feet and grabbed my purse.

"What do you mean you have to go? You just got here!" Natasha cocked her head to the side and stared up at me.

"I forgot about movie night with Trent."

"Oh, I definitely understand. But you have been so busy lately. We miss you, Cee." She poked out her lip.

"I will do better next time. Sorry."

"Yeah, have fun," said Rachel, and I could have sworn I saw her roll her eyes when I turned to give one last quick wave then headed for the exit.

***

The next day at work was a refreshing release. I navigated through the day with ease, playing and being goofy with my students, exploring concepts they had never seen, and watching their little eyes light up with each new discovery. Most people hated Mondays, but I looked forward to them.

On my lunch break, I headed to the teachers' lounge to grab a cup of coffee in preparation for round two. I had a little pep in my step – my kids had that effect on me. I sauntered over to the Keurig machine humming one of my favorite jams from the 90s.

After my cup was filled with liquid perfection, I made my way over to a seat, grabbing a granola bar from the snack basket before I sat down.

"Mmm," I intoned, relishing the sweet blend of chocolate and granola. I washed it down with a sip of coffee, and my insides began to thank me. I had begun craving these little delights ever since the school switched to this new brand. I always made sure I was the first one in the lounge so I could get one before they ran out. I drummed my fingers on the wooden table, contemplating my next move.

Just then, my heart leapt when I saw Trent enter the room, his eyes searching for half a second before they rested on me. I shot him an inquisitive smile, then I saw the brown paper bag in his left hand and the single red rose in his right.

My heart melted. "You are so sweet." I stood to meet him as he approached. We shared a brief kiss, then we sat down.

"I figured I would bring you lunch, especially since I fell asleep on our movie last night." He opened the bag to reveal my favorite: Jamaican style oxtails and white rice, with extra gravy and some plantains.

My eyes widened as my mouth began to water. "You can fall asleep every Sunday if this is how you make it up."

He chuckled in response. "Enjoy." He slid a carryout container over to me along with plastic utensils and ample napkins. He then opened his own container filled with his favorite: curry goat with white rice, no plantains.

We were silent for few moments as we savored the delicious tastes and aromas of our food.

"So, how's your day going?" Trent took a sip of his Pepsi then focused his attention on me.

I looked at him for a long moment – really looked at him like I hadn't done in a while. *I don't even realize what I have.* A lump formed in my throat. I smiled to mask my true emotions. "It's going good. After lunch I'm teaching a lesson about different animals around the world."

His eyes beamed with pride. "My baby – look at your sexy self. I always knew you would be a great teacher."

I blushed and smiled, but my expression changed when I looked past Trent to see Camron enter the room. My heart immediately began to palpitate as I fought to maintain my composure in front of Trent while not totally avoiding eye contact with Camron.

Act casual, I reminded myself.

He stared at me, then at Trent, before curling up his lip and shaking his head. Trent must have felt his eyes, because he quickly turned to see what or who had caught my attention. "Hey, brother … Camron, right?" He reached out his hand to shake Camron's. They had met at a teachers' luncheon a year ago, but didn't really know each other. Usually, Trent couldn't get away from the office, but that year, he'd made it a point to attend the luncheon with me. You can probably imagine how that day went.

Camron returned the gesture then said, "Catch you later, Cee."

My ears were hot as Trent turned back to me.

Trent closed his container and returned it to the bag. "Listen, baby, I gotta get back to the office. I hate to cut our lunch short, but I have back-to-back meetings with clients today."

"Oh, I definitely understand." I smiled, the temperature in my ears cooling off as I calmed down. My husband was dedicated to his job as an accountant, plus it was tax season, so I knew he had to be overbooked. "Don't work too hard."

I stood to kiss him goodbye as he folded the paper bag that contained the rest of his food and drink.

"If I do, you gonna help me relax when I get home?" He licked his lips and stared me up and down, sending chills up my spine.

"Don't get me in trouble at work." My voice was barely above a whisper – he knew how to take me there.

"I'm trying to get you to have my babies, girl," he drawled in a voice that was low enough for only me to hear.

"See, that's where it starts." I playfully nudged his arm, though his last statement caused the chills to immediately dissipate.

He kissed me again, not seeming to notice the difference in my demeanor. "I'll see you tonight." He winked then exited the lounge.

***

I sat back down in my seat, absorbed in thoughts of my marriage with Trent, which was swiftly approaching six years. We met in college and immediately fell in love. He worked at a factory doing hard labor – the strength and sexiness of his hands still showed it, though he left the company for an accounting firm straight out of college. They paid his way through grad school, but not before he asked me to marry him. We were well off, and the only thing he wanted from me was a baby.

I stared at the red rose, lost in thought.

"Have his babies?" Camron sneered, and I practically jumped in my seat because I'd forgotten he was still in the lounge. I glanced at him then craned my neck toward the hallway to ensure that Trent was out of earshot.

"You were listening in on us?"

"How could I not? You were broadcasting the whole thing right here in the teacher's lounge! If it had gone on any longer, you would have been arrested for indecent exposure!"

I blew out a short breath. "Cam, stop being so dramatic! And why did you even come in, knowing you saw us sitting here? Are you trying to get us both killed?"

"Now who's being dramatic? You know that soft ass nigga ain't about to do shit."

I snorted. "Says the schoolteacher."

"At least if I was the one who was your husband, we would have time to see each other!" He gestured between me and himself as he spoke. "What was that, twenty minutes, tops? Your lunch break is not even half over!"

"Look, don't make comments about something you don't know." I lowered my gaze to let him know not to go there, and I fiddled with the rose on the table.

"Listen, Cee, I don't know how much longer I can see you with him like this. We've been in a full-blown relationship for three whole years. You keep promising me you're gonna leave him, and I want to know when."

I didn't have a good answer for that. "It just hasn't been the right time." I wrapped up the rest of my lunch, my appetite long gone. I grabbed the rose and stood up, hoping to return to my classroom to regain at least ten minutes of solace, but Cam grabbed my arm. His eyes were filled with passion and fire.

"I love you, Cee." He emphasized his words. "I want to marry you. How much longer you gonna make me wait?"

I swallowed a new lump that had formed in my throat. "Just give me some time." My eyes couldn't withstand the intensity of his gaze any longer, so I looked at the floor.

He gently released my arm and took a step back. "Yeah. Okay."

I escaped from the room before either of us could utter another word.

***

With Xaveon, things weren't as complicated. I could mostly be free when I was with him, because his only requirement with me was that I kept it one hundred about my relationship status.

"I don't do married chicks, so if you married, we can stop this before it even starts," he told me right before we slept together for the first time. I told him I had a boyfriend named

Camron, but that it wasn't really serious. I kept him completely in the dark about Trent, all because I wanted to see what it would be like to have a man with dreads.

Xaveon was so sexy with his black dreaded hair that went down to his waist, his dark chocolate skin, and his alluring persona. I was immediately drawn to him the day my best friend Natasha introduced us.

Her eyes were beaming with pride, but I was fighting to keep the lust out of mine. Later on that night, I shot him a friend request. I had debated whether I should do it initially, because I didn't want Natasha to be suspicious, but when I saw that he was already friends with Rachel, our other best friend, I figured it would be okay.

My mouth practically watered at his pics, each one sexier than the last. I was careful not to 'like' or comment under any of them, though, because I didn't want Trent or Camron to see, much less Natasha. He accepted my friend request a few hours later, then he inboxed me the next day. Three days after that, we started meeting up.

I knocked on Xaveon's door, quickly glancing around to ensure that no one I knew could see me on his front porch. I always parked in the back behind his house to try to throw things off a little, but still, you could never be too careful. I waited for a few moments after I knocked, but he didn't answer, so I knocked again. Still, no answer. I was starting to get impatient, because Xaveon was like a drug, and I needed my fix, so I twisted his doorknob, and to my surprise, the door opened.

I quickly walked inside and closed the door behind me. It was pitch dark. "Xay, where are you?" I whined, pissed off that he was playing games.

Almost immediately, I felt his rough hands grab me and throw me against the wall. I opened my mouth to scream, but I was silenced by his aggressive kisses as he tugged at my clothes and lifted me up. I smiled in the dark, knowing that what was about to come would be well worth the anticipation.

After our session, we slept, and when we woke up, I decided to take the plunge and tell him about Cam, but of course I didn't reveal the true nature of our argument.

"Xay, what should I do?" I whined.

"Well, if the nigga wants you to marry him, what you waiting on?" Xaveon was so matter of fact in everything he said. That was one of the things I enjoyed about him.

Well, for starters, because I'm already married! But I certainly couldn't tell him that.

"You wouldn't miss all this?" I gestured toward my naked body.

"I mean, yeah, but you already know how I roll."

I was ready to swirl my neck with serious attitude, but then I remembered my own predicament. "So, don't you feel any guilt about what we're doing?" Natasha's face flashed across my mind.

"Do *you*?" His response was a little too sarcastic for my liking.

"So none of this affects you at all?"

"I'm not the one sleeping with some random dude behind my boyfriend's back. You really need to find another way to sort out y'all problems."

I wrenched away from him and sat up in the bed, holding the covers against me, suddenly aware of my nakedness though it hadn't mattered moments before. "You really got a lot of nerve!" I spat, but my conscience screamed, *So the hell do you!* "So, Natasha's not your girlfriend?"

He sucked his teeth. "I don't know why all y'all females got this fairytale image in your minds about how niggas really are. We do us, period. And clearly, y'all do y'all too." He gestured between me and himself for emphasis.

"So you're not even serious about her?"

"We kicking it, but she's not really my type."

"So, why are you with her, then?"

"Why are you with your boyfriend?"

"Don't turn this around on me."

"I'm not. I'm trying to open your eyes to see that the same bullshit I'm on, you on."

I didn't really have a response for that, especially since Xaveon didn't know my whole story. If he ever found out about Trent, I knew all bets would be off. He didn't "do" married chicks, which was, strangely, the only form of morality he seemed to adhere to.

I sighed and shrugged my shoulders, conceding that he was right.

Chapter 2

I laid in the bed staring at the ceiling, our crisp white comforter pulled up to my chin. The walls in our bedroom were blank, like they were filled with secrets, much like my life. I listened to the water running in the bathroom that adjoined our bedroom as Trent finished his shower. Tax season caused him to have to go into the office today, though it was the weekend.

A lump formed in my throat as I thought about how hard-working, faithful, and loyal Trent was, which starkly contrasted my own character. I swallowed it, knowing that I had made this bed a long time ago, and I was sure to have to lay in it, sooner or later.

I jumped slightly as the shower water abruptly turned off. I heard him fumbling through the bathroom, probably drying himself off and preparing to shave. Trent was so predictable, but in a good way. I always knew what to expect with him. He worked, he provided, he attended to my needs, and he let me have my freedom.

Hmm. Maybe the fact that he let me have so much freedom was a bad thing.

About ten minutes later, he emerged from the bathroom wearing nothing but his boxers and a white A-shirt. I had to pause my thoughts to take in his sexiness. His skin was smooth and milk chocolate, like a Hershey bar.

Saying 'yes' was easy for me when he first proposed – I only had eyes for him. But now that we had been married for five years, with our sixth anniversary swiftly approaching, I was wondering if we should have waited. Maybe we married too young.

"Good morning, beautiful." He leaned down to kiss me on the lips. I don't know why he insisted on kissing me every morning, even when my breath probably smelled like something had curled up and died in the back of my throat, but that was what he wanted, so I obliged. His breath was minty fresh, and he smelled like that new Versace cologne I bought him a few weeks ago. "What's wrong?" he said, his expression full of concern.

"Nothing."

"What're you going to do today?"

I scooted over in the bed so that he could sit down and look at me as he pulled on his pants and slid into his shoes. I mustered up as dreamy an expression as I could. "Probably lay here all day thinking of you and missing you."

That caused him to smile, such a sweet, tender expression that my heart panged.

"Why don't you hang with Rachel and Natasha? Maybe you guys could go to the spa or something. You need some money?" My heart warmed. He was always trying to give me money, even though I had my own.

I sat up holding the comforter around my naked body. I shuddered at the eerily familiar scenario. This was essentially a repeat of the other day with Xaveon. "That sounds like a good idea, but I got it."

"Okay." He stood up to put on his shirt and jacket. I helped him button it up, then he clipped on his tie. That had been a fight during our first year of marriage – he preferred clip-on ties, while I thought regular ties looked more professional.

He ended up winning the debate when he told me that the reason he hated regular ties was because when he was younger, he was bullied by the older guys in his neighborhood, and one of the ways they bullied him was by tying a tie around his neck, holding him down, and squeezing until he cried. After I heard that story, I never bothered him about it again.

"Hoo-wee! Let me get a picture." I quickly grabbed my phone from my nightstand. He stood there bashfully as I went to my camera app.

"Do you have to do this every single morning?" He hated taking pictures, but I had hundreds of them stored in my phone. I just loved how he looked in a suit, and I suspected that unconsciously, I took so many pictures of him because I wanted to hold on to the good times while they lasted. I snapped the picture, then he came over and kissed me again. "I'm going to miss you too," he whispered, his voice husky.

"Boy, you know you have to go to work. Didn't you get enough last night?"

"I never get enough of you."

He pulled back then stared at me, looking me up and down. "I can't wait till you have my babies."

As soon as he said those words, a chill ran up my spine. I was going to have to find a way to turn this thing around, and soon.

***

I sat up in the bed at Camron's house, scrolling down my timeline as he slept next to me. I held my phone with one hand while I fingered my ends with the other. I was going to have to visit the salon soon. They were starting to split, and I also just wanted something different. Maybe I would cut it all off. I took in Camron's features as he lightly snored … caramel skin, slanted eyes, masculine lips, and a solid, stocky build. I didn't like to compare him to Trent, but if I had to say, he was a close second.

"Hey, sexy," he breathed, his eyes still closed. I was surprised that he was awake so soon. We had just spent the past few hours tumbling around in the bed, and now his eyes told me that he was looking for more.

"Hey."

He yawned and wiped his eyes, then a droplet of water from his cheek. I had showered after he fell asleep, and washed my hair in the process.

"What time is he supposed to get off work?"

I rolled my eyes at his tone. I hated when he spoke about Trent like that. Like it or not, the man was my husband, and he was going to have to show him some respect. "Why do you want to know, Cam?"

"Because I want to spend the whole day with you."

"Well, we can't. I have plans with Natasha and Rachel." I lied. I really just didn't want to deal with him pressuring me all day to leave Trent. It was like a never ending saga with him. I knew it wasn't fair, but Cam didn't know how to give a girl a break.

He sucked his teeth. "Don't they have their own men to hang out with?"

"Natasha does, but Rachel doesn't." *And that's probably for the best, seeing my track record.* I was becoming more and more entangled in this web. It was starting to choke me, and I desperately wanted out, but I didn't know how without hurting someone I loved. I suddenly felt nauseous as waves of emotion came over me.

"Babe, we really need to talk about this."

"Not today, Camron."

Trent and I had longevity. I truly loved him, but did I love him more than Camron? Did I even love Camron at all? Or did we just share similar interests? This was all so confusing.

"Ce'Anna, you're killing me. You keep going off in a little daze while I'm trying to talk to you about our future." His eyes were narrowed, and his jaw was on edge. That caused me to snap.

"I keep telling you, it's not that easy!" I spat. "You know Trent and I have been married almost six years. I can't just throw him away like he doesn't mean anything."

"But he doesn't mean anything when it comes to *us*, Cee." His eyes and voice pleaded with me. He sat up and gently cupped my chin with his hand. "Look at what we have. We're perfect for each other. Once you leave him, we can get married. Then you can truly be happy."

I stared at him for a few moments, assessing the anguish in his eyes. I shook my head, slowly scooting away from his embrace. "I just need more time to think."

He opened his mouth like he wanted to argue with me further, but then my stomach lurched as vomit rushed up to my throat. I quickly jumped up from the bed and barely made it to the bathroom before I released my insides in the toilet.

I felt Camron behind me, holding my hair back as I heaved. I hated throwing up, but eating sushi often made me nauseous afterward, though I loved it. That was what we had for lunch.

My eyes filled with painful tears as I stood up. *Why does life have to be so hard?* I brushed my teeth, then turned and practically jumped out of my skin when I saw Cam leaning against the doorway. I had forgotten he was there that quickly.

"You okay?" His slanted eyes expressed his concern.

"Yes, but I gotta go home. I'm not feeling well today."

"Let me take care of you."

"I can't." My voice trembled. "I just need to get home."

He nodded like he understood, then followed me back down the hallway, staring at me longingly as I put on my coat and shoes. I couldn't bring myself to look him in the eyes as I said goodbye, knowing where I was headed.

***

I had barely got in the door from my session with Xaveon when my phone rang with a call from Rachel.

"Hello?" I said, trying not to sound as irritated as I felt. I just didn't want to be bothered right now.

"Listen, Ce'Anna, I'm going to be brief, but you need to listen very carefully to every word that I'm about to say."

I stood still in the middle of my living room, not even bothering to take off my coat. "What is it?"

"You're sleeping with Xaveon. Don't deny it. I know it, and you're doing it behind Natasha's back."

My heart dropped. *How does she know?*

"What are you talking about?" I said, keeping it cool.

She sighed. "Cee, there's no point in playing this game. I saw you enter his house the other day, and I sat there until you came out two hours later. Your hair was all messed up, and your shirt was buttoned incorrectly. You didn't even try to cover up your shame."

"Geez, Rachel, stalker much? What were you even doing in his neighborhood?"

"It doesn't matter what I was doing there, Ce'Anna! What matters is that you are betraying our best friend. You are also betraying your husband. Does Trent have any idea that you are cheating on him?"

"No."

"Well, he's inevitably going to find out, as soon as you tell Natasha."

"Rachel, no! I can't tell her! I'll stop seeing him. Please, just don't say anything!"

"I'm not going to say anything. You are. You have seven days." *CLICK.*

***

I stewed in my emotions for a few hours after the phone call with Rachel. It was making me so anxious my head was starting to spin. *This is the beginning of the end*, I kept thinking, over and over again. I had to get myself together before Trent came home. I was supposed to be cooking dinner tonight, and I knew he would be starving by the time he came home. I quickly whipped together some spaghetti and garlic bread, then threw a cake in the oven. Those were some of this other favorite foods. *Oh my God, he's going to leave me!*

I had never allowed the thought to enter my mind before, but now it hit me. There was no way that Trent would stay with me after he found out about Xaveon, and I shuddered to think how he would feel if he found out about Cam.

I needed someone to talk to, but obviously, neither of my girls was an option. I grabbed my phone from the counter to call Xaveon. He may be blunt, but at least he spoke the truth.

Before I could even fix my fingers to go to his name in my contacts, my phone began to buzz and ring with a call from him. I swiped my finger across the screen. "Hello?" I was practically breathless.

"So this is how you keep shit one hundred?"

What could he be talking about? I just left his house! "What's wrong, Xaveon?" I was heated. I needed someone to talk to, and he was calling me with drama.

"Natasha just popped up at my house after you left, calling herself surprising me. You lucky she didn't see you. But that's beside the point. The fuck she mean, you got a husband?"

"What?" My mind was swimming. "What are you talking about?"

"She came to my house to have sex, then she started flipping through her phone talking about rings. That's when she made the comment that she wanted one similar to the one your *husband* Trent got you."

"Xay…"

"What the fuck did I tell you, Ce'Anna? I told you before we even started dealing with each other that I don't fuck with married chicks. That was my only rule, and you broke it."

"Xaveon, wait. Let me explain."

"Explain to your husband and your boyfriend. Lose my number." *CLICK.*

My hands trembling, I called him back, but he had already blocked me.

Chapter 3

Three days later, and I still have no idea how I'm going to get out of this. Trent and Camron both keep asking me what's wrong, but I have no idea what to tell them. I got an email from my job a few days ago about a weekend retreat. Before, I wasn't really interested, but now, I want nothing more than to go.

I'm suffering from withdrawal due to my break-up with Xaveon, if you can even call it that. I guess I didn't realize how much significance he played in my life. I relied on his advice way more than I knew, and now that he was out of the picture, I had no one to confide in.

I went back through my emails to find the one about the retreat. Once I found it, I tapped the screen to get to the website. I hoped that they hadn't filled up all the slots, and was relieved to see they hadn't.

Before I could tap the 'sign up' button, my screen lit up with a call from Rachel. I desperately wanted to reject it, but if I did, there was no telling what she would do. I answered reluctantly.

"Hello..." I sighed as if I was acknowledging my impending doom.

"I'm assuming you haven't done it yet, because Natasha hasn't said anything."

"Why are you so hell-bent about this?"

"How would you feel if you found out *your* best friend was sleeping with your man behind your back? I can't believe you did this, Ce'Anna! Do you even realize the heartbreak you are about to cause? Natasha is in love with that man, Cee. You already have a husband, but you couldn't just be happy with that. You had to go and take her man too."

"It was a mutual decision!" I regretted the words as soon as they came out of my mouth.

"A mutual decision, huh? Well you got four days." *CLICK.*

This was becoming a pattern – me saying something completely stupid, then someone hanging up on me.

When was it all going to end?

***

I awoke from my deep slumber when I heard the front door close. Trent was home. I quickly whipped my head toward the alarm clock. I must have slept all day! I didn't even remember getting into bed. All I remembered was being extremely tired after that conversation with Rachel. Her words played over and over in my mind until I finally drifted into an exhausted deep sleep.

"Hey," said Trent. He slipped off his shoes and gently kicked them into the closet; then he started on his jacket, coat, and tie.

"Hey."

"Did you cook?" He glanced at me as he stepped out of his pants. He was now down to his boxers and A-shirt.

"No, I'm sorry. I fell asleep."

"It's okay. I figured you were knocked out when you didn't answer my call earlier. I know you haven't been feeling well lately."

My heart stung at the sweetness of his concern. He went into the bathroom to take his shower, and I lay there with tears streaming down my face. How could I cheat on this man? All he cared about was making me happy, and look how I returned the favor.

I wiped them away, and picked up the phone to order us some food. That was the least I could do. The place I ordered from was pretty quick, and the food arrived right when Trent was exiting the shower. I paid the driver and brought our meal to our room.

"That was quick," Trent chuckled, as he brushed his 360 waves in front of the huge mirror attached to our dresser.

"I know, right! I'm so hungry. Guess I worked up an appetite, huh."

"Yeah, all that laying in the bed is so exhausting…" He chuckled and leaned down to kiss my cheek.

"Grab those trays for me," I said, as I opened the brown paper bag to take the food out.

"You got it. I smell Chinese food!" He set the trays in the sitting room area of our spacious master suite. "That's just what I had a taste for." He grabbed some cans of soda from the mini-fridge we kept in there for times just like this when we didn't feel like leaving the bedroom to eat a meal.

Settled next to each other on the love seat, Trent said, "So aside from your tiredness, how you been feeling?" He forked a mouthful of noodles.

"Not too good at all," I answered truthfully.

"I guess you not in the mood to try to make some babies tonight, huh?"

I could barely meet his eyes. "Not really. I'm sorry."

He nodded, then his expression turned slightly serious. "Hey, do you ever wonder about your biological clock?"

This time, I did look up at him. "What do you mean?"

"I know we're not old or anything, but we've been married almost six years. Both of our parents keep asking for grandchildren. You know I want kids, and I thought you did too. Before you know it, we'll be thirty. Are you still not ready?"

I opened my mouth to formulate an answer then closed it when I realized that I had no answer to give him.

"I mean, we don't have to try tonight. I understand you're not feeling well. But still, I feel like we've been avoiding this conversation for a while. Do you even want kids?"

"I don't even know, Trent. We both have so much going on with work. Kids would be a huge interruption in our lives, especially mine."

"I understand that, but you've got tenure at your job. I'm in a good place at mine. We have enough in our savings to at least get started. Why are you so hesitant? I'm not good enough to make babies with? You think I won't be a good father – is that it? You know what, it seems like something is always bothering you lately, and you can't be honest enough to just come right out and tell me. Talk to me. I'm right here. I'm your husband. I love you."

"You know, I'm really not up for this conversation right now. I literally just woke up when you came home. Can we come back to this later?"

He stared at me for a few moments, and his shoulders visibly slumped in defeat. "Okay, Ce'Anna. Whatever you want."

***

This is all just a big mess. I can't stop thinking about Xaveon, Cam is still breathing down my back, and I'm hurting Trent so bad that it's making me physically ill. I only have two more days until Rachel's deadline is up, and she does whatever it is she plans to do if I don't confess to Natasha. I told Trent I was going on the teachers' retreat that Friday and Saturday, and he reluctantly agreed to let me go.

I arrived at the location ready for a true escape. I saw a few teachers from my school there, and a few from other schools in the area. Thankfully, there was no one there that I really talked to, so I would mostly have time to myself.

I made sure not to tell Camron that I was going. He kept asking me about it, saying that this would be a way for us to slip out for a brief vacation, but I told him I would think about it, and I dropped the subject after that. Thankfully, he never brought it up again.

"Welcome!" the hostess chirped, greeting me a bit too cheerfully for my liking. She finalized my room reservation, her nails clicking noisily on the keyboard, and gave me my room key. I could not wait to get away from all these people. Everybody was getting on my last nerve right now. I planned to take full advantage of everything the spa had to offer, and I was going nowhere near any of the group activities.

By the end of the two days, I felt refreshed enough to go home Sunday morning. I didn't know what would await me when I got there, especially since my time was up with Rachel, but I figured that I would just have to take life as it came.

Chapter 4

The first thing I saw when I pulled up to my house was Rachel and Natasha's cars in the driveway, and my heart pounded with anxiety. I could imagine them sitting in my living room smug and angry, waiting for me to enter the lion's den. Trent's car was gone.

I didn't know what else to do, so I just got out of my car, grabbed my suitcase, and made my way to the front door, my head and heart pounding with every step.

The door flung open, and there stood Natasha, blocking the entrance to my own house. "Oh, so you gonna just act all nonchalant, like you not sleeping with my man, bitch?" She jumped toward me, but Rachel held her back, and we all stood in the doorway glaring at each other.

"No, we gotta talk about this, remember?" said Rachel, peering out to see if any of the neighbors were watching.

"Let's go in the house," I said. "Can I just set my luggage down?"

"Yeah, we can go inside," Natasha spat. "You taking a long weekend, Spa Queen, while I'm sitting here fuming about you taking my man! What you got to say about that?"

Natasha jumped at me again, and this time, she was successful. She knocked the suitcase from my grip, and before I knew it, we were rolling all over the floor raining blows on each other. We knocked down a lamp and almost broke one of the legs of my dining room table from falling against it so hard. Rachel tried to break us up, but it was no use. We were both too full of aggression to be stopped.

"HEY! What's going on here!" It was Trent's deep booming voice, and I heard bags drop to the floor as he rushed over to pull us apart. He grabbed Natasha while Rachel grabbed me. Natasha had a long scratch running down her face, and I could only imagine what mine looked like.

We stared at each other, panting.

"What the hell is going on here?" Trent repeated, his eyes traveling between all of us, then a look of horror coming over his face as he took in all the damage we had done.

"Ask your fucking wife!" Natasha shouted, then she jumped toward me again, but Trent held her back.

"Natasha, chill! You guys are best friends. Why are you fighting?" Trent's a strong man, but even he struggled to keep that wildcat in his grasp.

"Evidently, you don't know that your wife is a sneaky, manipulative little THOT!" Natasha tried to jump toward me again. "She been fucking my man since we got together." Her voice trembled at those last words, then she broke down sobbing.

Trent dropped her like she was a venomous snake. He stepped back in shock, his eyes widening as he looked at me.

Rachel also let me go, and I stood there, trembling, as Natasha cried on the floor.

There were tears in Trent's eyes. I could see him swallow hard before he trusted himself to speak. "Ce'Anna, is this true?"

I could practically hear my own heart shatter. I nodded, but I couldn't meet his eyes.

Rachel decided she'd had enough. "We're done here," she announced, and she helped Natasha out of the house without another word.

Trent stood there stunned, and then, needing something to do, he went to the kitchen to grab a broom. I watched as he swept up the glass, the hard expression on his face one that I had never seen before.

"Trent…"

"Don't." He roughly scraped some glass into the dustpan then released it into the trash can. He tried to sweep up some more, but the gravity of the situation hit him, and he flung the broom and dustpan across the dining room. "Fuck this shit!"

I didn't know what to say. I didn't know what to do. So I sat there on the floor in a miserable heap and braced myself for the onslaught.

"So you been sleeping with this guy for what, a month? Two?" He ran his hand down his face like he was trying to contain his rage.

"Yes."

"Is he the only one?" He walked over and crouched down in front of me then gently lifted my face so that I had to look at him. "Is he,

Ce'Anna?" His eyes pleaded for me to say yes, but I couldn't lie to him anymore.

"No." It barely came out in a whisper.

He let out a breath like he had just been punched in the chest. "No?" He stood up again and paced the living room, but when he stopped, he looked at me with such stone cold hatred, I could have sworn I saw his eyes change from brown to black.

"Who else." It was a statement more than a question.

"Trent…"

"Who else, Ce'Anna!" I could see the veins in his neck. I didn't know what he would do when he found out, but I knew I had to tell him.

"Camron."

He blinked again. "That teacher at your school – the one we saw the day I came and ate lunch with you?"

I nodded again.

"How long?"

I didn't want to say it, but I knew I had to. "Three years." I literally held my breath and waited for the hammer to come down.

He just stood there glaring at me, not saying a word, and then he started pacing again. I could see his adrenaline rising with each step he took.

"Trent…" I said, and then he hauled off and punched a hole clean through the wall, causing me to jump back in shock and the front door to shake from the impact. He snatched up his coat and banged out the front door, not even bothering to close it behind him. I watched him as he got in his car and screeched out of the driveway, headed to Lord knows where.

I stared at all the glass as my head began to throb from the day's events. The broken pieces represented all the broken trust, all the broken promises, all the shattered hopes and dreams.

Out of nowhere, vomit surged up from my stomach to my throat, and I ran to the bathroom, but not before I tripped over a side table and cut my hand on a piece of glass. I made it to the toilet in time, but getting my insides on the floor was the least of my worries.

My husband was gone, and my life as I knew it was over.

***

After three days, I still hadn't heard from Trent. I called him and called him, but he never answered his phone.

He finally got his wish, or at least maybe he did. I was pregnant.

I hadn't paid attention to all the signs, all the nausea, the mood swings, the headaches, but now, the truth was here, and it was almost too much to bear.

I prayed the father wasn't Xaveon, and I didn't even want it to be Camron's. Trent was the one who deserved this child. If I could give him nothing else, this would be my parting gift.

I felt like a zombie at work. I tried to keep it together for the kids, but this whole situation was just unbearable. I told Camron what happened with Trent, but I didn't tell him about Xaveon. I guess I was trying to hold on to whatever was left of my dignity, even if it was only a façade.

Camron tried to comfort me, but I could tell that he didn't give a damn about Trent.

"It's good he knows now," he explained. "Now we can finally be together."

But I don't want YOU! I want Trent. I need Trent.

I was home alone again on day five – still no word from my husband.

At around midnight, I heard someone creeping through the house. My eyes popped open and my heart gripped with fear. I prayed we weren't being burglarized. I had no kind of weapon. I grasped in the dark for my alarm clock, figuring I could at least throw it at the thief's head, but then Trent flipped on the bedroom light.

"Where have you been?" I gushed, jumping up to greet him, but he held out his bandaged hand to stop me from coming closer.

"I'm just here to get some of my stuff." His eyes were bloodshot, and his shirt was wrinkled.

"Trent, I'm so sorry."

"Yeah, I bet." He rummaged through the closet for his suitcase. He began packing some of his clothes and shoes.

"How long are you staying gone?" I was desperate to talk to him, to see him, to feel him.

"Forever."

"You can't mean that."

"Yeah?" He zipped up his suitcase and flung it over his shoulder, but it fell to the floor. He shook his head, cursing his clumsiness. He pulled out the extender and grabbed hold of it to roll the suitcase out of the room.

"How's your hand?"

"Oh, now you give a damn about me?"

"Trent, I'm pregnant." I knew this was totally an inappropriate moment, but I was desperate for him to stay.

He stepped back like I had slapped him in the face.

"You are a real piece of work. You know that?"

With those words, he made his way out the door.

My heart sank as I slid back onto the bed, my entire body feeling numb.

Epilogue

It's been a year since that night Trent packed his bags. We're divorced now. I tried everything to make it up to him, telling him that we could finally have what we always wanted: a family. He ignored all of my advances, and stated in no uncertain terms that the only association he would ever have with me would be if the child growing in my belly were his.

Those words burned, and my heart broke even more when I found out a month ago that he has a girlfriend now. It turned out that the child was his, and I tried to get back with him once again during my recovery from childbirth, but it was no use.

We had a son. I named him after his father.

When Camron found out the child wasn't his, he was kind of hurt, but he still wanted to be with me. I don't know what the hell was wrong with him – if Trent left, why didn't he?

***

Trent Jr. is six months now, and he is growing so fast. He is constantly trying to walk and talk, and anybody with eyes can see that he is Trent's pride and joy. Trent got engaged to that woman he was seeing, and they are planning to get married soon. I wanted so bad to tell him he was moving too fast, but I knew I had no room to speak.

Camron started pressuring me after Trent got engaged for us to finally move forward too. I didn't want to do it at first, but then I thought about the fact that he was literally there for me every step of the way, so I finally gave in.

We moved in together. Trent sold our old house. I got my half of the money, but money didn't mean anything when it came to all the memories we shared there.

Camron is a great stepdad, and truly a loving and attentive man. I wish I could say he made me forget about Trent, but my heart still burns for him.

Before you go…

If you enjoyed this quick read, please know that I would really appreciate a positive review on Amazon. Thank you so much! ☺

Also, if you would like to read more of my work, or hear more about me as an author, feel free to join my email list at https://www.tanishastewartauthor.com/contact, or follow me on social media:

Facebook: Tanisha Stewart, Author

Reader's Group (FB): Tanisha Stewart Readers

Instagram: tanishastewart_author

Twitter: TStewart_Author

Want more books by Tanisha Stewart? Turn the page!

Tanisha Stewart's Books

Even Me Series
Even Me
Even Me, The Sequel
Even Me, Full Circle

When Things Go Series
When Things Go Left
When Things Get Real
When Things Go Right

For My Good Series
For My Good: The Prequel
For My Good: My Baby Daddy Ain't Ish
For My Good: I Waited, He Cheated
For My Good: Torn Between The Two
For My Good: You Broke My Trust
For My Good: Better or Worse
For My Good: Love and Respect

Betrayed Series
Betrayed By My So-Called Friend
Betrayed By My So-Called Friend, Part 2
Betrayed 3: Camaiyah's Redemption
Betrayed Series: Special Edition

Standalones
A Husband, A Boyfriend, & a Side Dude
In Love With My Uber Driver
You Left Me At The Altar
Where. Is. Haseem?! A Romantic-Suspense Comedy
Caught Up With The 'Rona: An Urban Sci-Fi Thriller

#DOLO: An Awkward, Non-Romantic Journey
Through Singlehood

Made in the USA
Las Vegas, NV
07 November 2022

58890608R00031